Dear Parent:
Your child's love of reading starts here!

Every child learns to read in a different way and at his or her own speed. Some go back and forth between reading levels and read favorite books again and again. Others read through each level in order. You can help your young reader improve and become more confident by encouraging his or her own interests and abilities. From books your child reads with you to the first books he or she reads alone, there are I Can Read Books for every stage of reading:

SHARED READING
Basic language, word repetition, and whimsical illustrations, ideal for sharing with your emergent reader

BEGINNING READING
Short sentences, familiar words, and simple concepts for children eager to read on their own

READING WITH HELP
Engaging stories, longer sentences, and language play for developing readers

READING ALONE
Complex plots, challenging vocabulary, and high-interest topics for the independent reader

ADVANCED READING
Short paragraphs, chapters, and exciting themes for the perfect bridge to chapter books

I Can Read Books have introduced children to the joy of reading since 1957. Featuring award-winning authors and illustrators and a fabulous cast of beloved characters, I Can Read Books set the standard for beginning readers.

A lifetime of discovery begins with the magical words "I Can Read!"

*Visit www.icanread.com for information
on enriching your child's reading experience.*

I Can Read!

BEGINNING
1
READING

Pinkalicious®
and the Flower Fairy

To Kayla

—V.K.

The author gratefully acknowledges
the artistic and editorial contributions of
Daniel Griffo and Jacqueline Resnick.

I Can Read Book® is a trademark of HarperCollins Publishers.

Pinkalicious and the Flower Fairy
Copyright © 2019 by Victoria Kann

PINKALICIOUS and all related logos and characters are trademarks of Victoria Kann. Used with permission.

Library of Congress Control Number: 2018947895
ISBN 978-0-06-267567-5 (trade bdg.)—ISBN 978-0-06-256701-7 (pbk.)

20 21 22 LSCC 10 9
❖
First Edition

Pinkalicious®
and the Flower Fairy

by Victoria Kann

HARPER

An Imprint of HarperCollinsPublishers

"I want a flower fairy
to visit my garden!" I said
to my brother, Peter.

7

"I want a worm

to visit my garden," Peter said.

"Yuck!" I said.

I sprinkled seeds over our gardens.

"Flower fairies love
pink flowers," I said.
"Worms love mud," Peter said.
I raked and watered my garden.
"VROOM!" Peter yelled.

I worked hard on my garden.

After two weeks, my seeds sprouted.

There were little leaves

but no flowers.

The next day it rained and rained.

It rained for weeks.

When the sun finally came out,

I ran outside to see my garden.

"Now all my plants will bloom!"

There was a lot of green.

"Where's all the pink?" I wondered.

"ZOOM!" Peter said.

He drove his truck

through his garden.

He made roads with his shovel.

"Calling all worms!" he said.

"Take a ride on my racetrack!"

I had an idea.

I needed to show

my flowers how to grow!

I made tissue paper flowers

and put them in my garden.

"Calling all flowers!" I said.

"Bloom like these paper flowers!"

I waited all day,

but nothing happened.

How would I ever see a flower fairy

without any real flowers?

I was too sad to garden.

The next day, Peter yelled,

"Guess what I saw!

Hint: it was pink!"

"A worm?" I groaned.

"No," Peter said.

"A flower fairy!"

"No you didn't . . . did you?" I gasped.

"A PINK flower fairy?

Why didn't she visit me?" I said.

"My garden is better,"
Peter said proudly.
I looked at his garden
and looked at mine.

Peter was right.

I had to do something!

"I'm going to pinkafy my garden,"

I told Peter.

"Then the fairy will want

to visit me!"

Molly came over to help.

We strung sparkly pink lights

and shiny pink streamers.

We added a pink parasol

and set out pink fairy cakes.

My garden was a pink wonderland!

21

I put on music,

and Molly and I danced like fairies.

It was very loud, very fun,

and VERY pink.

Still the fairy didn't come.

All we saw was a wiggly pink worm.

My mom looked out the door.

"It's time to clean up," she said.

We began packing my pink belongings.

Soon my garden was plain again.

It was time for Molly to go home.

"We didn't see a fairy," I said.

Molly gave me a hug.

"Don't be sad," she said.

I sat down in the grass.

A big weed tickled my foot.

I pulled it out.

Behind it was a pink flower!

I pulled out more weeds.

I couldn't believe it!

My garden was beautiful.

There were flowers hidden

among the weeds all along!

I smelled a fragrant pink flower.

"Hello," said a little voice.

I was nose to nose with a fairy!
She was pink and shimmery.
She had flower petal wings.
"I'm very glad you cleaned
up your garden," she said.
"Now I have room to fly!"

"Your garden is pink perfection,"
said the fairy.

"There's just one thing that will
make it better."

29

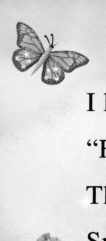

I knew exactly what that was.

"Fairy magic!" I cheered.

The fairy fluttered her wings.

Sparkles rained down.

More flowers grew and bloomed,
making a beautiful arch.
"Wow!" Peter and I said.

It was flowertastic!